The Universal Zoo

The Conservation Place at the Far End of Space

*To the memory of Mum (for the many trips to the library)
and Dad (for the many bedtime stories).*
N. Z.

To Jon and Lorna
W. H.

Text copyright © Neal Zetter 2022

Illustrations copyright © Will Hughes 2022

Designed by Steve Wells

First published in Great Britain and in the USA in 2022 by Otter-Barry Books

Little Orchard, Burley Gate, Herefordshire, HR1 3QS

www.otterbarrybooks.com

A catalogue record for this book is available from the British Library.

ISBN 978-1-91307-440-1

Illustrated with line drawings

Set in Stempel Schneidler

Printed in Great Britain

9 8 7 6 5 4 3 2 1

The Universal Zoo

Poems by **NEAL ZETTER**

Illustrations by **WILL HUGHES**

Otter-Barry BOOKS

Contents

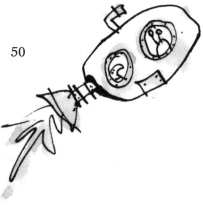

What's Where

1. Spaceship Parking
2. Entrance
3. Deep Dark Caves
4. Universal Café
5. The Keeper's House
6. The Gigantic Lake
7. Exit and Gift Shop

Universal Zoo Guide

Welcome!
Roll up!
Come on down
to the Universal Zoo.
Want to see amazing animals?
Buy a ticket, join the queue.
Preserving them,
conserving them,
that's what we do.
Every creature has a place
at the far end of space
in the Universal Zoo....

Space Hound

He's a space dog
In his space home
Eats his space treats
Chews his space bone

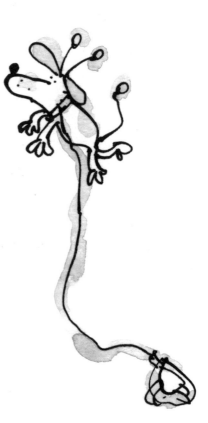

Makes his space woof
When he space talks
On his space lead
Goes for space walks

Stops on space grass
For his space wees
Loves to space scratch
Itchy space fleas

Chases space cats
In his space sky
Watches space birds
When they space fly

Never Feed the Gronk

Never feed the gronk
If you hope to keep your head
Never feed the gronk
Even if he's just been fed
Never feed the gronk
Unless you choose to lose your limbs
Never feed the gronk
Unless you're seriously dim

He'll definitely harm ya
Although you're wearing armour
Never, never, never feed the gronk

Never feed the gronk
Terror teeth that cut like knives
Never feed the gronk
I saw him eat two people's wives
Never feed the gronk
Unless grave danger rings your bell
Never feed the gronk
Unless you walk the road to hell

With appetite voracious
And stomach super-spacious
Never, never, never feed the gronk

Never feed the gronk
Don't dish dinners near his jaws
Never feed the gronk
Don't leave lunches by his claws
Never feed the gronk
Unless you're heavily insured
Never feed the gronk
Cos once you're dead there is no cure

Feed hay to hungry llamas
Feed leaves to giant iguanas
Feed monkeys ripe bananas
Feed sharks and feed piranhas
But never,
     never,
          never feed the gronk!

The Worry Fish

He's in a state of panic,
tormented and distressed,
continuously anxious
and constantly depressed.
He's radiating anguish
and riddled with self-doubt,
the first to find an issue
to agonise about.
He can't help his genetics,
but if he had one wish
he'd be a salmon, skate or hake
and not a worry fish.

His middle name is Nervous,
he lives a life perturbed,
tried tai chi and tried yoga,
yet still he's so disturbed.
He's splishing, splashing, shaking,
when pained or plagued or vexed.
You ask him, "What's the problem?"
He'll scratch his head, perplexed.

It's how his brain is wired,
but if he had one wish
he'd be a lamprey, loach or roach
and not a worry fish.

He worries about friendship,
the world economy,
what food to choose for breakfast
and drowning in the sea.
He worries that he's healthy
or far too fat or thin.
His greatest fear is one day
he could stop worrying.
It's how he was created,
but if he had one wish
he'd be a pilchard, plaice or dace
and not a worry fish.

The Unknown

It can't meow
Or claw and scratch
It's clearly not a cat

Not long and thin
It doesn't squirm
It's probably not a
worm

It doesn't growl
Grow fur or hair
Conclusion: not a bear

No bumpy hump
Upon its back
It's plainly not a yak

It sleeps all night
Can't dig a hole
I guess it's not a mole

It doesn't leave
A slimy trail
Unlikely it's a snail

It's skinny, blue
With purple wig
So maybe not a pig

Can't hear a quack
Can't hear a cluck
It's neither hen nor duck

It has no spout
No fins or tail
It's surely not a whale

It won't chew hay
Or carrots cos
It's definitely not a
horse

It doesn't make
A mooing row
I'm doubtful it's a cow

What's this weird creature
In the zoo?
Nobody knows – do you?

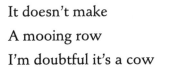

Martian Kids

Martian kids
Oh so cool
Martian kids
Five feet tall

Martian kids
Got two heads
Martian kids
Got three legs

Martian kids
Dress real weird
Martian kids
Grow long beards

Martian kids
Mauve and blue
Martian kids
Have tattoos

Martian kids
Use jet packs
Martian kids
Eat ear wax

Martian kids
Breathe green gas
Martian kids
All hate maths

Martian kids
Play with rocks
Martian kids
Chew their socks

Martian kids
Hide in caves
Martian kids
Misbehave

Martian kids
From the stars
Martian kids
Come from
MARS

The Shy Shimmereen

The shimmereen sits,
covering her eyes,
quivering,
quaking,
shaking.
The shyest of the shy.

A sphere of silky fur,
an orange ball of fluff,
a tiny timid type,
filled up and full of nervous stuff.

The shimmereen stands
two centimetres tall,
peering,
peeping,
peeking,
while hiding from us all.

When hopping through the grass
or skipping over ground
she rarely makes a noise,
so quiet you hardly hear a sound.

The shimmereen eats,
snacking on her food,
nibbling,
chewing,
gnawing,
still tucked away from view.

And as night-time arrives
she stretches out to sleep
in soft marshmallow bed,
the gentlest creature you could meet.

The shimmereen sits,
covering her eyes,
quivering,
quaking,
shaking.
The shyest of the shy.

Jumbo Fleas

Jupiter's 6.5-metre-tall jumbo fleas have a
strange and permanent problem...

Jumbo fleas have cats
They're jumping everywhere
Jumbo fleas have cats
They're swinging from their hair
Creatures cling onto their bodies
People stare at them real oddly

Jumbo fleas have dogs
Complete with canine homes
Jumbo fleas have dogs
Their kennels, leads and bones
Animals always attacking
Itching, itching, scratching, scratching

Jumbo fleas have mice
Their enemy within
Jumbo fleas have mice
Creep-crawling 'cross their skin
Try and try but they can't shake them
When they travel have to take them

Jumbo fleas have rats
So seldom sleep at night
Jumbo fleas have rats
Bite, nibble, nibble, bite!
Hop around in deep frustration
Vets prescribe strong medication

Jumbo fleas have goats
Infesting their hard shells
Jumbo fleas have goats
And all their kids as well
Parasites stick to each torso
Cats, dogs, mice, rats, goats and also

Jumbo fleas have
Jumbo fleas have
Jumbo fleas have...

FLEAS!

The Ticklelix

A creature that laughs more than any
other in the Universe

She's fun and full of laughter
No animal is dafter
Lives happy ever after
The ticklelix

Each time that you approach her
To cuddle, pet or stroke her
She howls just like a joker
The ticklelix

She grins and smirks and sniggers
And shrieks and screams and snickers
Then often wets her knickers
The ticklelix

Outrageously guffawing
Hilariously roaring
Not dull or drab or boring
The ticklelix

Her tummy jogs and jiggles
Her middle always wriggles
Emitting whoops and giggles
The ticklelix

She's neither mean nor bitter
Cos she's been born to titter
Which creature's a side-splitter?

The ticklelix

The Last Grizzzard

The last one of her species,
soon to be no more.
Ruined homes, habitats,
hunted by the score.

A sweet and gentle creature,
peaceful, tranquil, calm,
who wandered on wild open plains,
incapable of harm.

Once grizzzards grazed in multitudes,
numerous and plenty.
But... today...
their breeding grounds are empty.

She cannot understand it.
Disappearing friends,
family lost, vanished,
too much to comprehend.

The sun is sadly sinking,
setting on this beast.
A star in nature's history,
extinguished and deceased.

Once grizzzard herds were numberless,
measureless and many,
but tomorrow a feature of the past
because this grizzzard...

is the last.

The See-Through Throom

There's a species on exhibit
So astounding and amazing
You can scan his body's innards
As they're readily displaying

With skin totally transparent
Watching him's like watching telly
You can peer into his brain and
You can peek into his belly

See his adenoids, appendix
See his eyeballs via his nostrils
See his ligaments and liver
See his ear-holes, see his tonsils

You can spot his heartbeat throbbing
You can spy his food digesting
And his reproductive system
Is extremely interesting

See his bowel, see his bladder
See his pancreas and pharynx
See his corneas and kidneys
See his lungs and see his larynx

He's a number one attraction
Join the queue to get a viewing
Such an entertaining creature
Look at him and see right through him

The Snoralotz

The snoralotz does nothing,
but lies around and snores.
Some say she is exhausted,
some say she's really bored.
For every passing moment
a zed falls from her nose
while she flops there in underwear
with head between her toes.

The snoralotz is snoozing,
inactive, oh so tired.
Both nostrils keep vibrating
as life fails to inspire.
She cherishes her sack-time,
would love to hibernate,
drop off and doze and then repose
from morning until late.

The snoralotz is dormant,
deep sleeping very still.
The doctor made a visit,
concerned that she was ill.

Once creatures thought her lazy
or possibly stone dead,
till she replied, "My ideal day's
Unconscious in my bed."

The snoralotz is resting,
lost in the land of dreams,
and forty winks, she'll tell you,
beats chocolate and ice cream.
The snoralotz is napping,
flat-out upon the floor,
enjoying crashing, comatose,
cos she just wants to...

snorezzzzzzzzzzzzzzzzzzzzzzz.

No Such Thing as Dragons

I said, "Dragons?
Dragons! DRAGONS!?
Do not exist,
only found in fairy stories,
fiction, fantasy and myths."

I said, "Dragons?
Dragons! DRAGONS!?
There's no such thing,
just in tales of knights in armour,
magic, castles, queens and kings."

I said, "Dragons?
Dragons! DRAGONS!?
Don't make me laugh.
Giant creatures spitting fire,
how ridiculous and daft.

So what is this...

Flame-breathing
Lung-heaving
Wing-flapping
Jaw-snapping
Tail-lashing
Teeth-flashing
Man-eating
Earth-heating
Foot-stomping
Rock-chomping
Stone-squelching
Smoke-belching
Town-torching
Ground-scorching
Sky-flying
Meat-frying
Claw-scratching
Egg-hatching
Flesh-ripping

Blood-dripping

Beast...

Standing in front of me?"

**ROOOOOOOO
OOOOOOOOAA
AAAAAAAAA
AAAAAR!!!!!!!**

Dodo, Dodo

*The dodo, a (supposedly!) flightless bird, disappeared
from Earth many years ago. But they are actually alive
and well in a galaxy far away...*

Did you know know
We are dodos?
We're still here here
Didn't go go
Please stop telling us that we're extinct
It's a lie lie
Do not cry cry
We're not dead dead
Didn't die die
More alive than everybody thinks
Cos we fly fly
In the sky sky
Into space space
Soaring high high
Though the experts never thought we could
In this home home
We now roam roam
Special place place
Dodo zone zone
If you're passing visit our neighbourhood

Hear us talk talk
Hear us squawk squawk
We're not hens hens
We're not hawks hawks
We make positively perfect pets
With big beaks beaks
We're no freaks freaks
Beady eyes eyes
Funny feet feet
We have certainly not disappeared yet

Dodo dodo
Dodo dodo
Dodo dodo
Dodo dodo
Dodo dodododo do do do
Dodo dodo
Dodo dodo
Dodo dodo
Dodo dodo
Dodo dodododo do do do!

The Kaleidoscoper

Crimson is the colour of his fingers
Tangerine's enlivening his nose
Peep beneath his shirt and vest
You can view his yellow chest
While a mix of teal and turquoise tints his toes

Mustard is the colour of his eyeballs
Ear-holes sink in never-ending black
Though it's very rarely seen
His spleen's shaded neon green
Stripes of pink and purple criss-cross down his back

Indigo's the colour of his elbows
Violet's looking lovely on his lips
From his rectum there's a light
It's a spectrum glowing bright
And a hoop of blue sits snugly round his hips

Lemon is the colour of his kneecaps
Auburn spots and dots adorn his head
Every colour you could see
Covers his anatomy
Why chase rainbows? Go to visit him instead

The Morph

This animal from the planet Krogle is the Universe's most incredible shape-shifter

He's a tree

He's a bear

He's a bag

He's a chair

He's a coin

He's a spoon

He's a rock

A balloon

He's a cup

He's a car

He's a laugh

Ha! Ha! Ha!

He's a pot
He's a plant
He's your grumpy old aunt
He's a key
He's a ring
He can be anything!

And so what is he now?
Can you guess?
Take a look
He is held in your hands...

He's this poetry book!

The Sludge

A wonderful weird creature
A muddy brown blob
Enormous amoeba
A soft spongy slob

A giant pile of jelly
A glow in the dark
With eyes like bright headlights
With teeth like a shark

She snorgles and she snutters
Spits balls of sour slime
While slinking in circles
A space Frankenstein?

Sprawled on the sharpest shingle
Halfway up a tree
She fartles and flubbers
And guzzles green tea

Each dinnertime it's pizza
Each lunchtime it's fudge
That's all that we know of
The life of the sludge

The Brain

He's the brain!
Yes, that's his name,
a creature with no body
or a skeletal frame.
How he evolved it isn't clear,
without a nose, mouth, eyes or ears.
He's certainly not from round here.

He's the brain!
A massive mind,
just pink pulsating jelly,
simply one of a kind.
An encyclopaedia packed
  with facts
who never ever
  sleeps or snacks.
Can't moo, meow,
  oink, bark, cluck, quack.

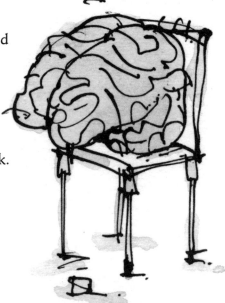

He's the brain!
Sits in his chair,
transmits transparent thought waves
through the alien air.
Unmoving seven days a week,
a telepath who is unique.
Renowned for wisdom not physique.

He's the brain!
Supremely smart,
his intellect, when measured
hits the top of the charts.
Much sharper than the sharpest pin,
throw your computer in the bin,
you won't need it if you meet him.
He's the brain!

Universal Limericks

Megatum Whales

All megatum whales from Poseidon
store ten thousand people inside them.
If you ask them why,
they'll let out a sigh,
saying, "We've nowhere else we can hide them!"

The Minimoo

The minimoo creature of Saturn
is tiny so frequently sat on.
To make herself taller
(and suaver and cooler)
she now walks round with a huge hat on.

X()&y S)_&y_) ppp&^v6@@*

ghjakga;lGka;kja;jntg;r/983(&_)
lrkAp'gjh240igix8r=]kjdh(
)(%£&UF^IE_)+>>F
ipf904tg04u10-r-2
opfj-80=9g=-g9g=e00gh^&$%)U

(*Traditional limerick about the vacuum fish of Draaal in original Draaal language)

The Ten-Legged, Swivel-Headed, Bushy-Bearded, Twirly-Tailed Horrox

This creature gained fame from a name
   so easy to forget
He strains hard to remember it but
   hasn't cracked it yet
Extremely long, he gets it wrong as
   you do too I bet
The Ten-Legged, Swivel-Headed, Bushy-
   Bearded, Twirly-Tailed Horrox

If you met him you'd probably find his
   introduction stalled
Cos every day he struggles to retain what
   he is called
He feels embarrassed, shameful, daft
   and frequently appalled
The Ten-Legged, Swivel-Headed, Bushy-
   Bearded, Twirly-Tailed Horrox

A definite world record top zoologists agree
The most titanic title in all animal history
While he signs just one autograph you'd swim
    the Seven Seas
The Ten-Legged, Swivel-Headed, Bushy-
    Bearded, Twirly-Tailed Horrox

When telling you his moniker he's breathless,
    out of air
The alphabet's exhausted with few letters
    left for spare
It's fine recalling parrot, penguin, pig
    or polar bear
But not The Ten-Legged, Swivel-Headed, Bushy-
    Bearded, Twirly-Tailed Horrox

The Keeper

*The Keeper is a super-intelligent android created
to run all aspects of the Universal Zoo*

I'm the Keeper, I'm the Keeper
Of this Universal Zoo
Looking after these rare creatures
Is what I was built to do

Watch me water them and feed them
Help and heal them when they're sick
And stay with them and play with them
Show them new and clever tricks

I have studied all their species
Books, statistics, data, facts
Know their habitats and habits
Where they live and how they act

I clean out their homes and paddocks
Give them big hugs if they're glum
I'm the rock they can rely on
Their pal, buddy, friend and chum

I'm their guardian, defender
Here protecting every beast
Sometimes parent, babysitter
Sometimes teacher or police

I'm the Keeper, I'm the Keeper
Of this Universal Zoo
Looking after these rare creatures
Is what I was built to do

The Brown Belch of Iko

A thousand stale bread crusts
Ten tons of worn tyres
Huge mountains of moon-dust
Four miles of steel wires
Fresh fungus from Titan
Washed down with paint thinner
The Brown Belch of Iko
Sits scoffing its dinner

The Far End of Space

Want to visit the Universal Zoo?
Here's where to find it:

A billion light years from the world of your birth
Try hard as you might you will not spot the Earth
The Milky Way's disappeared, leaving no trace
Magnificent and magical
The Far End of Space

Our dazzling sun is nowhere in the sky
Strange planets rotate while bright shooting stars fly
Moons, meteors, asteroids spin round this place
Fantastic and fabulous
The Far End of Space

The science you learnt counts for nothing up here
A nebula's glowing, two quasars appear
See supercharged rockets zoom past at such pace
Sensational and splendid
The Far End of Space

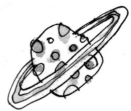

When travelling this way you must bring a map
Take just one wrong turn and you'll never get back
New uncharted paths for the whole human race
Beguiling and brilliant
The Far End of Space

The Invisible
Ballaboo Beast

The paddock's deserted,
abandoned and bare,
a thorough inspection
reveals just fresh air.
Has she vanished,
been banished,
or impossibly small?
No, the ballaboo beast is invisible.

Though tickets are purchased
and visitors queue,
there's huge disappointment
with nothing to view.
Has she darted,
departed,

or won't answer when called?
No, the ballaboo beast is invisible.

Nobody has seen her
since she first arrived,
perhaps playing hide-and-seek
or in disguise.
Has she quit,
escaped, split?
No, she's fooling us all
because...

the ballaboo
beast is

Can you see the...

Snaking

Slithering

Slinking

Sliding

Sidewinding

Shifting

Scuttling

Swaying

Swishing

Swirling

Swiping

Spinning

Stretching

Silver-striped

Scarlet-spotted

Scintillating

Sparkling

Shimmering

Shiny

Slobbering
Salivating
Spitting
Sniffing
Snuffling
Snorting
Spluttering
Squawking
Squealing
Screeching
Screaming
Squishy
Squashy
Squidgy
Squelchy
Spongy
Soft
Supple
Smooth
Slimy
Slippery

Super-strong
Smelly
Stinky
Stealthy
Sneaky
Sly
Secretive
Sensitive
Smart
Serious
Sensible
(Sometimes silly)
Superb
Special
Stunning
Startling
Stupendous
Sensational
Spectacular

...Ssassassarass?

The Simileon

She's...

As tall as a tree
As huge as a house
As fast as a falcon
As quiet as a mouse

As black as this ink
As sly as a fox
As fierce as a tiger
As strong as an ox

As wild as a wolf
But don't run away
Cos she's asking nicely
"Do you want to
play?"

This topsy-turvy lifestyle
leaves everyone confused.
His hats and caps fall to the floor,
he has no need for shoes.

To him it's not a problem,
to us it's rather strange.
He'll tell you Spain is north of France
and France is south of Spain.

He smiles each time you meet him,
but you'll think it's a frown
cos his whole world is back to front,
reversed, the wrong way round.

Perhaps on his own planet
all creatures are the same,
with legs forever in the air
as blood runs to their brains.

So if you spot this beastie
when visiting the Zoo,
make him extremely happy
and do a handstand too.

The Upside-Downer

Two feet are pointing skyward,
two eyes glare at the ground.
He spends his days the weirdest way,
just hanging upside down.

The Perfect Pet

Want to own the perfect pet
Best pet that you've ever met?
If you do then don't forget
You can't beat a guzzuggle

Such a caring, sharing chap
Snuggles, cuddles on your lap
Love and happiness on tap
You can't beat a guzzuggle

Let him nestle on your head
Cutely curl up in your bed
Purr profusely when he's fed
You can't beat a guzzuggle

Never scratches, never bites
Never screeches, never fights
Find the furry friend that's right
You can't beat a guzzuggle

Talk to him and he'll reply
Says hello and waves goodbye
Sociable so seldom shy
You can't beat a guzzuggle

Why opt for a coot or cow
Salamander, snake or sow?
Hurry to the pet shop now!
You can't beat a guzzuggle

The Enormous Egg

Who knows when it will open?
Who knows when it will crack?
Who knows when it will shatter?
Who knows when it will hatch?

Who knows what lurks inside it,
concealed within its shell?
They've studied it intensely
but scientists can't tell.

Who knows the place it came from?
Nobody has a clue.
Some say a flying saucer
that zoomed over the Zoo.

It stands at thirty metres,
bright blue with blobs of black.
Who knows which creature laid it
or if they'll want it back?

It's been there for a decade,
perhaps a longer time.
Occasionally it trembles,
sends tremors through my spine.

Who knows when
  it will open?
Who knows when
  it will crack?
Who knows when
  it will shatter?
Who knows when
  it will hatch?

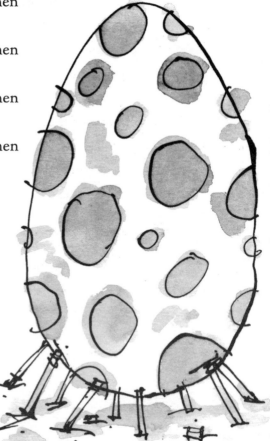

The Ordinary

She's an ordinary creature
From an ordinary place
Wears her ordinary features
On her ordinary face

With her ordinary body
Of an ordinary weight
She makes ordinary offspring
With her ordinary mate

She eats ordinary dinners
From her ordinary bowl
Builds her ordinary nest
Inside an ordinary hole

Loves her ordinary sleeping
In her ordinary bed
And her fur is ordinary
Coloured black, blue, white and red

She has ordinary pastimes
Doing ordinary things
Like her ordinary tricks
Upon her ordinary swing

She's boring, unspectacular
Dull, average and plain
Now you've met her you'll forget her
??????? is her name

The Zany Zakaloptofly

The zany zakaloptofly is wacky.
The zany zakaloptofly is weird.
The hat he wears is made of glass,
he sports a handlebar moustache,
two onion rings are hanging from his ears.

The zany zakaloptofly is crazy.
The zany zakaloptofly is odd.
He has a strange hypnotic stare,
collects old bits of underwear
and feasts on fresh fried gonga beans and cod.

The zany zakaloptofly is barmy.
The zany zakaloptofly's bizarre.
His right is left, his left is right,
asleep all day, awake all night
while swimming at the local cinema.

The zany zakaloptofly's eccentric.
The zany zakaloptofly's unique.
He gargles with ten piles of pins,
smears peanut butter on his skin
and plays himself at snap and hide-and-seek.

The zany zakaloptofly is bonkers.
The zany zakaloptofly is daft.
He whistles when you tug his tail,
talks backwards to his new pet quail
and drinks the water from his neighbour's bath.

The zany zakaloptofly is gaga.
The zany zakaloptofly is nuts.
I'm pleased to say he's now my friend,
so asked him how this poem should end.
He answered, "Bongo-boogie-hiccup-pyjamas-
blahblahblah-sausages-vacuum-cleaner."

The Wordy Bird

Check out the wordy bird
The wordiest bird yet
He learnt the dictionary
Memorised the alphabet

He loves to play with nouns
Experiment with verbs
Knows mighty powerful adjectives
A super language nerd

Eats anagrams for tea
Whole crosswords for his lunch
When feeling proper peckish
He'll find metaphors to munch

While resting in a tree
Or gliding through the sky
He'll read a whole thesaurus
Then give synonyms a try

In literacy at school
He proudly tops the class
Completing all exams and tests
With much more than a pass

He asked me how to rhyme
I showed him what to do
So yesterday I'm pleased to say...
He wrote this poem too!

Zooteacher

There's a teacher on display at the
  Universal Zoo
Doing everything schoolteachers do

Shouting at the dodos every time they squawk
Asking creatures not to run but
  "Walk! Walk! Walk!"
Showing the shimmereen how not to be so shy
Coaching the worry fish to smile instead of cry
Babbling with the ballaboo about the ABC
Hollering at Martian kids stuck climbing on a tree

She's such an incredible zoo exhibit
Of all the animals she's the best one in it

There's a teacher on display at the
  Universal Zoo
Doing everything schoolteachers do

Sitting in the straw on the floor on her own
Drinking coffee, playing with her mobile phone
Telling off the ticklelix for laughing too much
Yelling "Upside-downer – hey – hang the right
  way up!"
Setting very challenging homework for the brain
Helping the Ten-Legged, Swivel-Headed,
  Bushy-Bearded, Twirly-Tailed Horrox to
  remember his name

She's the first zooteacher that I've ever met
I want to take her home and keep her as a pet

There's a teacher on display at the
  Universal Zoo
Doing everything schoolteachers do

The Triangle Fish

She has three straight sides
Is a metre wide
You'll not find her high up in a tree
In oceans instead
Floating on the seabed
Pure one hundred and eighty degrees

Equilateral
So symmetrical
With the shape of a soft cheese spread too
If geometry
Isn't your cup of tea
She can calculate answers for you

Like a pentagon
She's a polygon
Count her corners now – one, two and three
Splish-splash, splish, splash, splish
Meet the triangle fish
The most fabulous fish in the sea

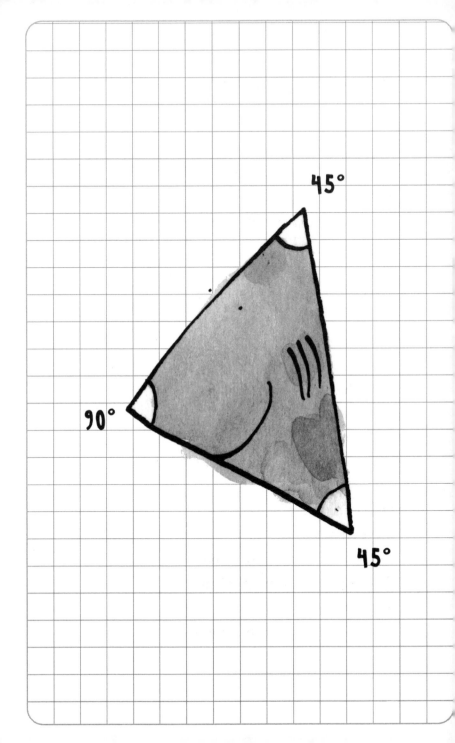

Catches space balls
Fetches space sticks
Sees his space vet
When he's space sick

Takes his space swim
In his space lake
Licks his space lips
For his space steak

Digs his space holes
In his space ground
Cosmic canine
He's a space hound!

The Spiral Spider

Did you spy the spiral spider
steadily sticking onto the glass?
Did you spy the spiral spider
swiftly scuttling through the green grass?

Did you spy the spiral spider
casually curling into a ball?
Did you spy the spiral spider
weirdly wandering over the wall?

Did you spy the spiral spider
carefully crawling across busy roads?
Did you spy the spiral spider
seriously scaring arachnophobes?

Did you spy the spiral spider
horribly hanging by a fine thread?
Did you spy the spiral spider?
No? Then search on the World Wide Web!

And Remember...

A message from the Keeper and Neal Zetter

Next time you're up in space
Next time you're flying by
Next time you're round this way – just stop!
View our place of conservation
Full of wonder, fascination
(And please make a small donation in our shop)

Next time you're travelling
Next time you're over here
Next time you're in our galaxy…
Say hello to every creature
We're sure they'll be glad to greet ya
Meet our marvellous and strange menagerie

Next time you're journeying
Near to our neighbourhood
Next time your rocket's passing through…
See the great work we are doing
Saving species and renewing
Pay a visit…

To the Universal Zoo!

Be a Universal Zoo Poet!

Now it's your turn to write a poem and draw a picture about a creature you'd like to see conserved in the Universal Zoo. Just grab a sheet or two of paper and follow these tips:

1 Think of a name for your imaginary creature. You might want to use it for your poem's title.

2 Take a few minutes to plan your poem by making some rough notes. These ideas might help you:

- What does your creature eat?
- What does it do?
- What noise does it make?
- What does it smell like?
- How does it move about?
- What does it like and dislike?
- Where does it come from?
- What's its shape?
- How big or small is it?
- What does it wear?

- What kind of personality does it have?
- What would its skin or fur feel like if you touched it?

3 Now start writing your poem but remember you do not have to rhyme, and if you do you may find it much harder than you think. Searching for one of the many rhyming dictionary sites on the Internet might help you.

4 Repetition of the title, a word or a line in the poem is also a very effective way to create a powerful poem.

5 Give the poem a clever ending so it creates a lasting impact. Maybe ask a question, use a pun or a smart twist.

6 Once you have written your poem read it aloud a few times, then edit and improve any parts that don't quite work. Be patient, as editing is the most important part of writing and you need to stick with it if you want your poem to shine!

Now you can draw and colour a picture of your creature on the same or another sheet of paper to make it really come ALIVE!

 Congratulations - you're now an official Universal Zoo poet!

About the Author and the Illustrator

Neal Zetter is an award-winning comedy performance  poet and entertainer, with a background in communication management and mentoring. He uses his interactive, rhythmic, rhyming poetry to develop literacy, confidence, creativity and communication in 3-103 year olds.

He runs his fun poetry writing or performance workshops daily in schools and libraries with children and adults all over the UK. He is the author of nine children's poetry books, but *The Universal Zoo* is his first collection for Otter-Barry Books. He lives in London.

Will Hughes is an illustrator and author of children's  books. He studied at Hereford College of Arts and has a degree in Illustration from the University of Edinburgh. In 2018 he was selected to be part of the Picture Hooks Mentoring Scheme, culminating in an exhibition at the Scottish National Gallery of Modern Art in 2019. Will works primarily in ink, but also uses watercolour with an element of collage. He has given workshops in primary schools and looks forward to more events in schools, libraries and bookshops across the UK. He lives in Malvern, Worcestershire.